Anne Fine

Tales from

WEIRD STREET

With illustrations by
Vicki Gausden

First published in 2017 in Great Britain by
Barrington Stoke Ltd
18 Walker Street, Edinburgh, EH3 7LP

www.barringtonstoke.co.uk

Text © 2017 Anne Fine
Illustrations © 2017 Vicki Gausden

A CIP catalogue record for this book is available
from the British Library upon request

ISBN: 978-1-78112-572-4

Printed in China by Leo

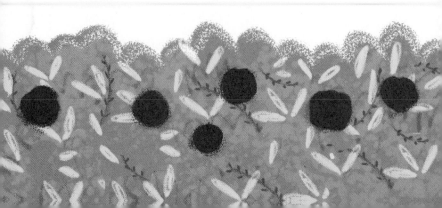

CONTENTS

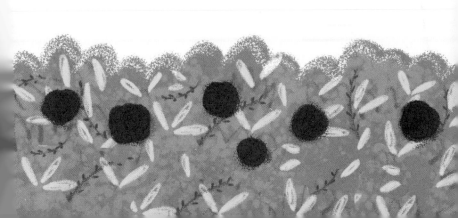

Our road isn't really called Weird Street. That's just what Asim and I call it. Its proper name is Weir Street because there is a stretch of the river at the end that plunges down, fast and deep like a waterfall, over the old weir.

Asim and I call it Weird Street because so many strange things happen here. We share the stories between us.

I told the first one that day. It was so hot. Asim was lying in the shadow of our garden wall. His sister Laila rocked to and fro on my old swing set. She had been staring at my great-grandpa, fast asleep in his deck chair with his old straw hat way down over his eyes.

"He doesn't talk much, does he?" Laila said.

"Sometimes he does," I said, and then I told them a story my great-grandpa had once told me.

Tale 1

The Family Photograph

Gramps and I were alone in the garden. Dad had gone off to get pizzas for later, and Mum was out with a friend. Gramps was slumped in the deck chair, and I was taking a break from the weeding. I sprawled on the grass to watch an ant haul a leaf across a bare patch. I'd just been telling Gramps about how one of the boys in the street had slipped off the river bank close to the weir, and almost drowned.

Gramps said, "That's how George Henry died."

I didn't know what to say. I knew that Gramps had a twin brother who'd died young. But no one talked about it. I didn't want to drag Gramps into saying more than he wanted, but I was curious.

Very curious.

"How old was he?" I asked.

"Not that much older than you are now, Tom."

I gave him a moment, then asked, "How did it happen?"

The answer couldn't have surprised me more.

Gramps said, "It was my fault."

I stared at him. "*Your* fault?"

He nodded. "In a way. You see, I'd had a warning."

"A warning?"

Gramps sighed. "The clearest warning. And yet I was too stupid and stubborn to see it for what it was. So I missed my chance to save my brother's life."

"What on earth happened?" I asked him.

Gramps shut his eyes, as if he was sending himself back down some inner path to the far past. At last, he said, "It was like this. My eldest brother William had been offered a job. But it was thirty miles away. Back then, nobody travelled such a long way each day to get to work. It wasn't possible. We all knew William would have to leave our family home, and rent a room nearer the factory."

"He didn't have a car?" I asked.

"Cars were only for rich people in those days. Our family never had that kind of money."

I'd heard a lot about how poor our family was back then, so I just waited for Gramps to get back to the story.

After a bit, he said, "My sister Beth was leaving home as well. She was about to get married. Her new husband's farm was even further away, and Mother said she felt as if her family was being scattered all over. She wanted a photograph. 'Before you all go,' she said. And then, of course, she looked at me because I was the only one in the family who had a camera."

"Really? The only one?"

"Things were so different then," said Gramps. "For people like us, cameras were almost as rare as cars. But I'd been in the local scout troop for years, and our Patrol Leader had a day job at a photographer's studio. He knew that I was keen to learn, so he gave me one of his old cameras and showed me how to take my own pictures and develop them."

"Was that hard?" I asked Gramps.

"Not if you knew what to do," he said. "You went into his special dark room and filled flat trays with the right mix of chemicals. You wound the film out of the camera, and dunked it in the first tray for an exact amount of time. Then you used tweezers to slide it into the next tray, and so on. Hey, presto! It was mostly a matter of timing – and being careful."

"And you were careful?"

"Oh, my word, yes!" he said. "Film was *expensive*. And so were the chemicals. Not like now, when you just press a button to get rid of photos you don't want! If you got things wrong back then, you wasted a good deal of time and money."

I left the ant to his task with the leaf, and rolled over on the lawn to watch Gramps as he went on with his story.

"So on the next dry day Mother arranged us in a family group. Mum, my father, William and Beth stood arm in arm in a row. My twin brother George Henry was on his knees in front of them. They left a space for me beside George Henry. I fixed the camera on the tripod and aimed it for the precious shot. I pressed the button for the ten-second delay, and rushed to kneel in my spot beside William."

"And everyone tried to be sensible and stay still."

Gramps chuckled. "That's right. We did the whole thing seven times over, so I'd be sure to get a really nice photo of us all, with nobody blinking or looking silly."

Then Gramps' smile faded.

"Go on," I prompted.

He took a deep breath. "Well, next day, I developed the roll of film. I was as careful as

I could be. I knew it was important because William had already said goodbye that morning and gone off to his new job on his bike. We knew he wouldn't be back for a long while. But when I looked at the first photograph, I saw that there was something wrong with George Henry's face. It had come out all blurry."

"Perhaps you'd dripped some other chemical onto the film by mistake," I said.

"That's what I thought. So I looked at the next shot. But that was the same. Everyone else's face had come out clear and smiling. But George Henry's face was just a pale, wavering blur – almost as if I'd been taking that bit of the shot under water."

"What about all the rest of the photos?" I asked.

"Exactly the same. Every last one of them. Seven shots, all carefully taken and carefully developed. And every one of them spoiled in exactly the same way."

13

"What did you do?"

"*Do?*" Gramps said. "There was nothing I could do, but I felt *terrible*. I felt as if I'd thrown away everyone's time and my mother's money. I felt as if I'd let her down by saying I could do it by myself, then getting things so wrong."

Again, Gramps went quiet. I waited. I watched the ants again. It seemed ages before he took up the story.

"So I blamed George Henry."

"You blamed your twin brother?" I said. "How?"

"I said he must have moved his head on purpose. I showed Mother how clear the faces of the rest of us looked. I said he must have counted down the ten-second delay, then shaken his head as fast as he could each time the shots were taken. I said he must have done

14

it on purpose, to spoil all seven photos in the exact same way. It wasn't *my* fault, I insisted. It was George Henry's. There was no other way it could have happened."

"What did your mother say to that?" I asked.

"She was so angry with him," Gramps said. "Back then, you know, every last penny was important. You weren't allowed to waste anything. That was almost a sin."

"Did George Henry fight back?"

"My heavens, yes. He argued and argued. And that's when I did something I have been ashamed of all my life. I told the worst lie. I said to Mother that, for all that I'd been facing forward, I'd half sensed and half seen George Henry shaking his head."

We were both quiet now. The longer I thought about it, the more I thought that was a lie I wouldn't want to carry with me all my life. I think I understood for the first time why Gramps had never in his life spoken about his twin brother.

I had to ask. "So what happened then?"

"George Henry lost his temper. He shouted at me, 'You tell her! Tell Mother that I *wasn't* doing that! Tell her the *truth*.' But I'd worked myself so far into the lie, I felt I had to stick to it. So I said nothing."

Gramps' face turned bleak. He suddenly looked even older.

"George Henry was so mad at me, he just ran off towards the river. Mum gathered up most of the photographs, but one had fallen to the ground. I picked it up to study it again. And that was when I realised that the face looking up at me as if from under running water was a real warning."

Now tears were streaming down the crinkled lines in Gramps' old face. "I ran towards the weir. I ran and ran. I'd never in my life run faster. Still, I was too late."

I broke the silence that followed. "George Henry had already slipped?"

"*If* he slipped," Gramps muttered grimly, and he shut his eyes. The moments passed. And then he said it once again, but oh, so quietly. "That's *if* he slipped."

There wasn't anything I could say to that. So I said nothing.

"That's creepy," Asim said. "Very, very creepy. A photograph that shows you what's going to happen ..."

"Weird," I agreed.

Laila gave the old swing a little push with her feet. "I know a story that's a bit like that. And like your great-grandfather's, it's quite true."

"How do you know it's true?" I asked.

"Because Mei told it to me."

Mei is Laila's best friend. She goes to our school and her parents own the Chinese restaurant at the top end of Weir Street, near the main road.

"Go on, then," Asim said. "Tell us the story."

So Laila began.

Tale 2

The Fortune Cookie

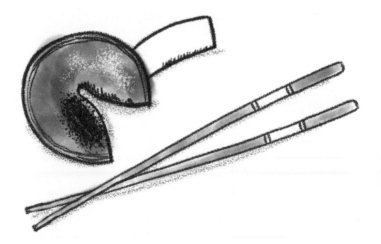

So, Laila told us, you know how Mei's older brother Huan works in their family restaurant almost every night. He's so cheerful and friendly, and brilliant at guessing what people who come to the Peach Garden might like to eat when they're not sure what to order.

So Huan's in the right place.

But Mei says the work's quite hard. And if Mrs Chang's assistant doesn't show up, Huan has to help in the kitchen, and he hates that. It's hot, it's steamy, and Mrs Chang starts off quite grumpy and then gets worse and worse as the evening goes on. She stands there, looking as if she's muttering evil spells under her breath into the saucepans and pots. Huan's always glad to finish on the nights when he works in the kitchen.

But mostly he just waits on tables. He takes the orders and brings them back to Mrs Chang. He carries out the trays of food. He tries to sort out any complaints, like –

"This isn't what I ordered. I said I wanted *duck*."

"This doesn't taste right."

"You didn't warn me it would have mushrooms in it."

"Why are there so few beansprouts?"

Sometimes he's surprised to get a tip at all. And sometimes he doesn't. That's why, when it's big parties of eight people or more, the Peach Garden add the tip to the bill before they take it to the table.

And then, one Friday night, something strange happened. Huan came to work at the normal time – 5.30 p.m. – because that's when the families begin to show up. And there were lots of them that night because it was the end of term and people were taking their children out for a meal for a treat.

Huan said they were terribly busy. He ran in and out of the kitchen with orders for two whole hours without a moment's rest. But by half past seven, most of the families were getting ready to go, or had already left.

Even then, Huan didn't get a break, because that's the time the groups show up. Lots of the people who work on Weir Street meet in the Riverside Inn for a drink after work. Then somebody gets hungry and says, "Anyone fancy moving on to a restaurant?"

Some people shake their heads and push off home. And some walk further along, to eat at

Spice Island. But most of them, Mei says, come into the Peach Garden.

Huan said he knew this group was going to be trouble from the start. They took for ever to get in the door. People were glaring at them because of the wind from the street. And they were so *noisy*. Huan offered them a table in the corner, but they insisted on a table in the middle of the restaurant. That wasn't helpful because the only one free was a table for six and there were seven of them. Huan had to pull up an extra chair. And one of the guys sat rocking back in it, getting in Huan's way. Mei said Huan got really cheesed off about that, because it meant that every time he had to carry dishes to the tables behind, he had to squeeze past, or go a longer way round.

It took these seven men ages to order. They changed their minds about a million times. And they all horsed about instead of choosing their food. One of them kept dripping soy sauce

in patterns on his paper napkin. A couple of them spun the salt pot across the table and back, really hard and fast, until the top flew off and salt went everywhere. Huan had to clear that up. And while he was doing that, they drummed out a tattoo on the table with their chopsticks.

You could tell everyone else in the restaurant was getting irritated, Huan said. Most of the other customers were watching, but nobody dared come over to ask them to behave. They weren't the sort of guys that you would want to argue with. Not on a Friday night – or any other time, come to that.

They settled down a bit as soon as the food arrived. But they kept being stupid – starting up chopstick fights and flicking bits of prawn or beansprout or noodle across the table. They thought themselves so clever, Huan said. But nothing he couldn't handle. And after a time the restaurant began to clear, as other people paid their bills and left.

Then things turned nasty. The man on the extra chair snapped his fingers to call Huan over, as if he was a dog. Then he demanded a dessert that wasn't on the menu. Huan told Mei that he'd never even heard of it. But this guy kept on shouting that it was a famous Chinese dish, and how could the Peach Garden claim to be a proper Chinese restaurant if they didn't serve it?

Then he started shouting that he wanted to speak to the chef.

Huan said that he got really nervous then. He didn't dare let this guy be rude to Mrs Chang. But Huan knew she had heard the racket because he saw her watching through the serving hatch, and it was clear that she was livid. Her lips were pulled as thin as matchsticks, and her eyes were glinting with anger.

Then, when this guy realised that the chef wasn't going to come out, he put on that pretend Chinese accent – you know, that mocking, sing-song voice that stupid people sometimes use, thinking it's funny. Huan told Mei he ignored that. He says the joke wears thin, even for idiots, and they soon stop.

And that's what happened. This stupid guy went on for a bit about how the chef couldn't be much good if the Peach Garden didn't serve this special dessert. Then he got bored and asked for the bill.

Huan brought it over to the table, along with the fortune cookies that everyone always has at the end of the meal.

Seven of them, one for each man at the table.

The rest of the guys broke open their fortune cookies, then shared the messages on the slips of paper inside like children reading riddles from a Christmas cracker. You know the sort of things they say –

"The dream you have will come true."

"Your life will be as free as the life of a flying bird."

"You will earn a great fortune."

Anything to send you out of the restaurant in a good mood.

This guy took the last cookie on the plate and broke it open.

Huan said it was the oddest thing. For the first time in all the years his parents had owned the restaurant, there was no fortune inside.

The man broke the shell and bits of cookie crumbled on the table. But there was no slip of paper with a message inside. No fortune.

Nothing.

And what was even stranger, Huan said, was that this guy didn't make any fuss at all. In fact, he went dead quiet. Just looked up.

That's when he saw Mrs Chang watching him from the kitchen. She wasn't hiding any more. She'd pushed the door wide open. And she no longer had that sour, thin-lipped look on her face. In fact, the opposite. She gave him what was almost a smile – and then a little wave.

Huan said she even looked friendly, as if she was waving him goodbye.

Then the man got up to leave. He followed his friends out. Huan stood at the door to watch them go off down Weir Street. And that's how Huan saw him stumble off the kerb, and under the wheels of that bus.

Just like that, Huan said. Under the wheels of that bus.

Huan said he turned to look at Mrs Chang. But she was nowhere near. She had gone back into her kitchen.

She was nowhere near.

Laila's story gave me the shivers. "Mei really told you all that?" I asked.

"She swore it was true," Laila said. "Horrible but true." She turned to Asim. "Your turn," she told him.

"I'm not sure my story's true," Asim admitted. "Do you remember Macie, whose family used to run the shop next to the Post Office? I heard it from her."

"Why do you think she might have made it up?" I asked.

"Maybe to pass the time?" Asim said. "You see, it was that day workmen were fixing a broken pipe under the pavement just outside their shop. Dad had sent me to buy eggs and I got in all right, but then the workmen started to shift a heavy barricade, so I was stuck for a while. There were no other customers. Macie was in there helping her mum and I think maybe she made the story up to pass the time because she was dead bored."

"We're dead bored too," Laila said. "So you can pass the time by telling us the story."

"Tell it exactly how she told it to you," I added. "Then Laila and I can judge whether it's true or not."

"All right," Asim said.

He sat for a moment, trying to remember. Then he began.

Tale 3

The Dream House

Mum and Dad used to tease me. It was because I always came down to breakfast with a great smile across my face.

My dad would ask, "Did you have the dream again, Macie? That dream about the beautiful house?"

I'd nod as I reached for the cornflakes packet. "Yes. I had the dream again."

"And is it still the same?" Mum would ask.

"Oh, yes," I'd tell them. "It's exactly the same as always. I dream that we are in the car and driving down a narrow lane. Tall trees arch above us, and at the end there is a hedge of wild roses. I get out and push open the gate, then I run up a mossy path to the most beautiful house. The front door is wide open, so I go in. I wander into the living room and pull back the heavy gold curtains to let in more sunlight. That's when I look out of the French doors and see a wonderful old wooden swing at the end of the garden. And it is swaying a little in the breeze and looks almost as if it's been there waiting for me."

That's when Mum and Dad chanted the words together, "And then you wake up!"

"And then I wake up," I agreed.

"You're always so *happy* in that dream house, Macie," Dad said.

"It's such a *nice* dream," I told him. "I run out into the garden as if I own the house. Sometimes I stop at the bed of lavender and squeeze one of the plant tops so I can smell its lovely scent. Sometimes I bend down and

there, right in front of me, I find a lucky four-leaf clover."

"And always, always," Dad said, "you wake up smiling."

"So would you," I told Mum and Dad, "if you could share my dream."

I'd watch both of them sigh. Then Dad would say, "But now we have to face the *real* day."

I'd watch Mum's face fall. Life's not been easy for our family. This shop's been robbed three times. Somebody scratched our van along both sides out of pure spite. And Mum reckons that almost every time she walks in our back gate, something horrible has happened. The heads have been pulled off the flowers in the tubs. Or someone has kicked over the bins and booted rubbish all over.

I must have heard her say it a million times – "I'm not sure I can face much more of living here."

And Dad would always answer, "How can we move? We have the shop to think about. A shop can't run itself."

I've always helped in the shop as much as I can. I like to help before I go to school and then again when I get home. I stack the milk cartons and yoghurts in the fridges. I put things people have decided not to buy back in the right places on the shelves. I even sweep the floors. If Mum looks tired, I like to surprise her with a cup of tea.

Sometimes in the morning, other kids come in and see me with the mop, cleaning up spills. "Hi, Macie," they say. "You skipping school today?"

"No," I say. "I'll be there."

I always am, too. I know exactly when to leave the shop to get through the gates in time. I'm never late. I love school – it's almost like a holiday, and we've never been on one of those. There's never been enough time or money. I think that's why I love my times on the swing in the dream house garden so much.

It's all so lovely and restful. Not like what Dad calls 'real life'.

On Saturdays, I help in the shop after I've been swimming and wandered back across town with my friends. In the evening it gets very busy. People come in to buy their lottery tickets. Everyone seems to have a set of special numbers they hope will bring them luck. Some of them even kiss their tickets before they tuck them away inside their wallet or purse.

"Maybe this week!" they say.

As soon as they were far enough away, my dad used to mutter, "You'll be lucky!" He always said that lottery tickets were a waste of money. He told me that 32 million people buy lottery tickets each week, and most of them buy three at a time!

"But only one person in 14 million is going to win," he added. "So it's like throwing money down the drain."

"Not for the two or three who win!" Mum pointed out. But she would never buy lottery tickets either. She'd say, "I'd rather get something real for my money."

But I was there the day the woman with golden hair came into the shop. She wore a flowery shawl that floated round her as if she'd brought a little breeze into the shop. She gave me and Mum the longest looks, almost as if she was inspecting us. Then she said, "One lottery ticket, please," and chose her numbers.

Mum started to print off the ticket.

Just at that moment I heard a clatter and Dad called, "Macie, can you help me with these tins of beans?"

I went off down the side aisle, out of sight, and helped Dad put all the tins back on the shelf. When I came back, Mum was still standing staring at the lottery ticket machine.

"What's up?" I asked.

"I don't know what to do," she said. "I'd just put in that woman's numbers when she vanished."

"Vanished?"

"Yes," Mum said. "Something went wrong with the machine. I looked down to sort it out and when I lifted my head, she'd gone. Just vanished."

"How odd," I said. "Perhaps she was in a hurry and got impatient."

"Perhaps," said Mum. "But now the silly machine refuses to cancel her numbers. It's got stuck."

"It can't *stay* stuck," I said. "Tonight's our busiest time."

"I know." Mum dipped in her pocket. "I suppose I'll have to buy the stupid ticket myself!"

She pressed the key that said 'FINISH', and the machine spat out the ticket with the numbers the woman had chosen.

Mum crumpled it into a ball and dropped it in the bin.

I dived to rescue it. "You never know!"

"I think we do, Macie." She laughed. "One chance in 14 million? Oh, I think we know."

Still, I unfolded the ticket and hid it in my pocket before Dad saw it and got cross with Mum for wasting money on the lottery.

*

We won.

Neither of them believed it, of course. I had to drag them in from the kitchen to look at the numbers. "See? They match," I almost yelled. "We've *won*."

It took for ever for them to be sure. They phoned up twice, in case it was a joke. The woman at the lottery admitted that it was the smallest jackpot in three years, and even then we had to split it with two other winners.

"Still," Mum said, "is it enough to buy a nice house somewhere in the country?"

The woman laughed. "Oh, yes," she said. "You'll have more than enough for that!"

So we've just sold the shop – and our old van – to my friend's uncle. He is delighted. So are Mum and Dad.

Now we can move.

The people from the lottery are good at giving advice. They found us Mrs Mears. She showed us round so many houses that it made our heads spin.

"I don't want anything too big and fancy," Mum said. "I would feel out of place."

"Or anywhere too small and poky," Dad said. "We've had enough of that."

I said I didn't care what size of house we had, so long as it had a garden.

Each day, Mrs Mears sent us photographs of houses, along with their details. Then she and Mum would meet up to make a list of the ones my mum and dad wanted to see. Sometimes I came along. One time, when I was with them, Mrs Mears picked up a photo, then shook her head and shoved it on the pile of rejects without a word.

"What's wrong with that house?" Mum asked her. "It looks nice."

"No, really," Mrs Mears said. "You don't want that one."

"Why not?"

Mrs Mears gave a nervous smile. "It's just that I wouldn't want you to end up in that house."

"Why not?" Mum persisted.

Poor Mrs Mears looked so embarrassed. "Because it's *haunted*," she said. "I shouldn't tell you that. It's my job to *sell* houses, not put people off them. The owner is called Mr Ford. His wife adored the place, but now she's dead, it's too big and he wants to move away. I know she'd think you were the perfect family to live there. But I'm told that strange things keep happening in that house and garden. I'd hate to think of your family going to all the trouble to move there, and then being scared and unhappy."

But Dad and Mum don't really believe in ghosts, so they insisted that we went to see it. We set off in the car. When we turned off the main road, we found ourselves driving along a leafy lane with branches arched above us.

All of a sudden I felt uneasy. I nearly said, "I feel as if I've been down here before."

At the end of the lane, where we parked, there was a hedge of wild roses. Mum and Dad stopped to admire them, but I couldn't help myself. I just pushed open the gate and started to run up the soft, mossy path to get to the open front door.

Mrs Mears was there, waiting. "Mr Ford is just finishing a bit of work in the greenhouse," she said. "But he asked me to show you around."

Mum and Dad followed her into the kitchen, but I knew that I had to go upstairs to see the bedroom Mum had told me might be mine.

I stepped in. It was bright and white and airy – the perfect room for me! And then the strangest thought came into my mind. It wasn't what you would expect.

It wasn't, 'I could be happy here.'

It was, 'I have been happy here.'

It felt so odd. I didn't want to be alone any more, so I ran back downstairs. No one was in the kitchen so I went into the next room.

Heavy gold curtains across the French doors kept the room in shadow. But one strip

of sunlight fell on the picture above the fire. A woman with golden hair and a flowery shawl was smiling down at me.

I whispered, "I remember you. You are the one who vanished from the shop and left the lottery ticket."

She only seemed to smile a little more.

I hurried to the French doors to tug the curtains open and let in more light. And there in the garden was the swing I'd seen so often, swaying in the breeze and waiting for me. There was the lavender bed I knew so well from my dream. And, when I started down the steps onto the lawn, the first thing I saw at my feet was a lucky four-leaf clover.

"I'm really here at last!" I whispered to myself. "I'm in my dream!"

Just at that moment, a man stepped out of the greenhouse at the bottom of the garden.

He saw me standing there and stopped dead in his tracks.

"You!"

"Yes," I admitted. "Me."

Just then, Mrs Mears came up behind. She saw us staring at each other and tried to introduce us. "Mr Ford, this is Macie. Her parents are just looking round."

"Oh, I know Macie," he said. "I have seen Macie in this house and garden many times before."

Mrs Mears looked astonished. "You've seen her before?"

"All the time," Mr Ford said. "She pulls aside those gold curtains and comes down the steps. She always stops at the lavender bed on her way over to the swing. Sometimes she reaches down and finds a four-leaf clover."

We smiled at one another as Mum and Dad walked over the lawn to join us.

Mum looked so worried. "I adore the house!" she said to Mr Ford. "I love it, and it's perfect for our family. I'm just not sure I'm brave enough to live in a house that some people think has a ghost."

"There can't be any ghost," I told Mum with another smile. "Not any more. Because I know I have come home."

"Well?" said Asim. "You've heard Macie's story now. Do you believe it?"

"That family did move away," said Laila. "And her friend's uncle does own the shop now. So that bit is true for sure."

"Perhaps it's all true," I said. "I wouldn't be surprised. Strange things are always happening on Weir Street."

They are, too. After all, that's why we call it Weird Street.

Our books are tested
for children and young people by
children and young people.

Thanks to everyone who consulted on
a manuscript for their time and effort in
helping us to make our books better
for our readers.